Poets From Essex

Edited By Catherine Cook

First published in Great Britain in 2019 by:

Young Writers
Remus House
Coltsfoot Drive
Peterborough
PE2 9BF
Telephone: 01733 890066
Website: www.youngwriters.co.uk

All Rights Reserved
Book Design by Spencer Hart
© Copyright Contributors 2019
Softback ISBN 978-1-78988-898-0
Hardback ISBN 978-1-83928-546-2
Printed and bound in the UK by BookPrintingUK
Website: www.bookprintinguk.com
YB0419I

Foreword

Dear Reader,

Are you ready to explore the wonderful delights of poetry?

Young Writers' *Poetry Patrol* gang set out to encourage and ignite the imaginations of 5-7 year-olds as they took their first steps into the magical world of poetry. With **Riddling Rabbit**, **Acrostic Croc** and **Sensory Skunk** on hand to help, children were invited to write an acrostic, sense poem or riddle on any theme, from people to places, animals to objects, food to seasons. *Poetry Patrol* is also a great way to introduce children to the use of poetic expression, including onomatopoeia and similes, repetition and metaphors, acting as stepping stones for their future poetic journey.

All of us here at Young Writers believe in the importance of inspiring young children to produce creative writing, including poetry, and we feel that seeing their own poem in print will keep that creative spirit burning brightly and proudly.

We hope you enjoy reading this wonderful collection as much as we enjoyed reading all the entries.

Contents

Jerounds Primary Academy, Harlow

Zack Godfrey (5)	1
Amelia Joshi (5)	2
Arda Mahmudov (7)	3
Oscar Davis (6)	4
Oscar Jonathan Rout (6)	5
Emelia Rebekah Martin (7)	6
Benjamin James Adamiec (7)	7
Ellie-May Burnall (6)	8
Harry James Early (6)	9
Sienna Weeks (6)	10
Jasmine Jenkins (6)	11
Yaaseen Idrees (7)	12
Blake Saunders (7)	13
Sheri Chen (7)	14
Annie Edgley (6)	15
Elijah William Rouse (6)	16
Maicy Mai O'Mara (5)	17
Lukas Dapsas (6)	18
Eleni Spearman (6)	19
Laci Jensen (5)	20
Malgorzata Sasak (6)	21
Henry James Hughes (6)	22
Amber Bishop (5)	23
Kirsten Osei-Yeboah (6)	24
Ananya Vyas (6)	25
Halle Grace Griffin (6)	26
Harry Cusack (7)	27
Pheobe Buckland (6)	28
Ryan Haddon (6)	29
Rose Weber (6)	30
Eddie Kemsley (6)	31
Millie-Rose Page (6)	32
David Marioara (6)	33
Alfie Chappell (5)	34
Dale Gould (5)	35
Harry George James Manoli (6)	36
Evie Joy Pollock (6)	37
Noah Daker (6)	38
Jack Downes (5)	39
Sophie Savory (6)	40
Azeem Idrees (5)	41
Caleb Edwards (5)	42

Jotmans Hall Primary School, Benfleet

Jessica Hagger (5)	43
Travis Nunn (6)	44
James Doré (5)	45
Dylan Crane (6)	46
Finlay Gow (6)	47
Adam David Smith (6)	48

Newtons Primary School, Rainham

Naomi Okafor (6)	49
Ioana Rebecca Vencu (6)	50
Muhammad Uzair Khan (6)	51
Jason Cibian (6)	52
Aaban Master (6)	53
Tiffany Bevan (6)	54
Iya Momprasert (5)	55
Yaqub Sadat (5)	56
Ibrahim Muhammad (6)	57
Leena Follad (6)	58
Ashton Waldrum (6)	59
Callum Bullman (6)	60
Bobby Scott (5)	61

Joanna Ephrem (5)	62
Isla Summer Leigh Angel Foster (5)	63
Sonny Antonio Pelosi-Davis (6)	64
Rishith Saha (6)	65
Ariana Pippa Ramsey (6)	66
Somto Ezeofor (5)	67
Daisy Mae Deitz (6)	68
Tyler Howard (6)	69
Tasfia Ruhee (6)	70
Seyi Oni (5)	71
Albie Ramsey (6)	72
Ayaan Rahman (5)	73
Amelia Ho (6)	74
Stanley Fitzpatrick (6)	75

Parkwood Academy, Chelmsford

Olaedo Ezinne Ugwoke (7)	76
Riley Antony Costello (7)	77
Harrison Banes (7)	78
Thomas Riley Roe (7)	79
Katie Gilbert (7)	80
Summer May Head (7)	81
Lucas Herman (6)	82
Ryan Clayton (7)	83
Finnly Alan Taylor (7)	84
Mikey Robert Mills (7)	85
Paige Jo Sargeant (7)	86
Archie Bark (7)	87

Ripple Primary School, Barking

Sid Albert Ward (6)	88
Maryam Imran Mansuri (5)	89
Emilija Lagunaviciute (6)	90
Kanishka Sarkar (6)	91
Ponam Kaur (6)	92
Bertille Ashley Okinyi (6)	93
Ayman Sochi (5)	94
Hamza Aslam Avram (6)	95
Sariyah Bashar (5)	96
Joshua Okine-Williams (6)	97
Ubaydah Noor (6)	98

Alessia-Maria Ciceu (6)	99
Hajar Khan (6)	100
Janelle Osei (5)	101
Aydin Bashir (6)	102
Aidan Muhammad Najib (6)	103
Malisa Begum (6)	104
Kobby Owusu Ansah (6)	105

St Teresa's Catholic Primary School, Rochford

Ruby Aimee Durrance (7)	106
Maisie Marshall (7)	107
Richard Clarence Henley Harris (7)	108
Aidan Ward (7)	109
Hannah Masiyambiri (7)	110
Jessica Morgan (7)	111
Ollie Griggs (7) & William Mortonson (7)	112
Zak Collins (7)	113
Quinn Beesley (7)	114
Amelia Lench (7)	115
Ronnie Harvey (7)	116
Joshua Tasker (6)	117
Kai Cundy (7)	118
Betsie Mahers (7)	119

The Poems

Beetle

I have a yellow and blue body.
I can walk fast and slow in the rocks and dirt.
I can be different colours, all of the colours or just plain.
My antennae look like horns.
I have bumps in my legs.
I have a bony body, head and tummy.

What am I?

Answer: A beetle.

Zack Godfrey (5)
Jerounds Primary Academy, Harlow

A Dragonfly

I have tall, long and bumpy blue legs that are skinny.
I have see-through wings that I glide on.
I have four black legs.
I have a long green tail.
I have big round eyes and a blue face.

What am I?

Answer: A dragonfly.

Amelia Joshi (5)
Jerounds Primary Academy, Harlow

What Am I?

I am soft, cute and furry.
I play around on the clean, green grass.
I have white ears to make me hear better.
I am hairy just like a hairy dog.
I run outside to play and have so much fun!

What am I?

Answer: A rabbit.

Arda Mahmudov (7)
Jerounds Primary Academy, Harlow

Bumblebee

My wings are white and delicate.
I am yellow and black in colour.
I can be fluffy.
I have six legs.
I eat flowers and pollen.
I am very good.
I am fast.
I can fly.

What am I?

Answer: A bumblebee.

Oscar Davis (6)
Jerounds Primary Academy, Harlow

Spider

I have long legs.
I have a fat tummy with a big shadow.
I am the colour black with orange.
I am furry and crawl about.
Sometimes, I am creepy.
I can be extremely fast but also slow.

What am I?

Answer: A spider.

Oscar Jonathan Rout (6)
Jerounds Primary Academy, Harlow

What Am I?

I have a long tail.
I am part of the cat family.
My skin is yellow with black spots.
I am the fastest on the planet.
I live outside.
I eat meat.

What am I?

Answer: A cheetah.

Emelia Rebekah Martin (7)
Jerounds Primary Academy, Harlow

What Am I?

I climb up trees.
I eat bananas.
I am friendly.
I play games.
I am very hungry all the time.
I am scared of gorillas, they are big.

What am I?

Answer: A monkey.

Benjamin James Adamiec (7)
Jerounds Primary Academy, Harlow

Sparkle Magic

I have a horn.
Everyone likes me.
I am magical.
I have glittering sparkles.
I am so bright that I stand out.
I look beautiful.

What am I?

Answer: A unicorn.

Ellie-May Burnall (6)
Jerounds Primary Academy, Harlow

Bumblebee

I have a fuzzy, stripy body which is white and thin.
I have wings that make me go fast.
I have sharp, spiky legs moving as sharp as a claw.

What am I?

Answer: A bumblebee.

Harry James Early (6)
Jerounds Primary Academy, Harlow

Bee

I am black and yellow.
I am fluffy and smooth.
I have a stripe-patterned body and clear wings.
I have matte eyes with shiny centres.

What am I?

Answer: A bumblebee.

Sienna Weeks (6)
Jerounds Primary Academy, Harlow

Butterfly

I have delicate, midnight black legs.
I have black and thin antennae that wiggle.
I have wings that are yellow, white, black and orange.

What am I?

Answer: A butterfly.

Jasmine Jenkins (6)
Jerounds Primary Academy, Harlow

What Am I?

I have black and white stripes.
I am gigantic.
I have a long tail.
I live in a stable.
I am fast and big.
I have soft hair.

What am I?

Answer: A horse.

Yaaseen Idrees (7)
Jerounds Primary Academy, Harlow

What Am I?

I live underground.
I come at night and sometimes during the day.
I can jump over people's gardens.
I eat whatever I find to eat.

What am I?

Answer: A fox.

Blake Saunders (7)
Jerounds Primary Academy, Harlow

What Am I?

I am soft, furry and cuddly.
I love outdoors or indoors.
I like digging holes.
I have long ears.
I like carrots and grass.

What am I?

Answer: A rabbit.

Sheri Chen (7)
Jerounds Primary Academy, Harlow

Spider

I have hairy legs.
I have eight eyes and eight legs.
I can spin webs.
I creep and crawl.
I have a black and orange body.

What am I?

Answer: A spider.

Annie Edgley (6)
Jerounds Primary Academy, Harlow

Worm

I have a pink and black tail.
I am wriggly.
I am slow and bumpy but delicate.
I have thin, little pink hairs.
I am clever.

What am I?

Answer: A worm.

Elijah William Rouse (6)
Jerounds Primary Academy, Harlow

Butterfly

I have black lines and a delicate, slim body.
I have white dots and a couple of orange dots.
I am colourful.
I am fragile.

What am I?

Answer: A butterfly.

Maicy Mai O'Mara (5)
Jerounds Primary Academy, Harlow

Spider

I have big, shiny, black teeth.
I have massive, black, spiky legs.
I have thirty soft red eyes.
I have a white sticky web.

What am I?

Answer: A spider.

Lukas Dapsas (6)
Jerounds Primary Academy, Harlow

Bumblebee

Bright yellow and stripy black
I collect pollen.
I fly like a roller coaster.
I make yummy, golden, sticky honey.

What am I?

Answer: A bumblebee.

Eleni Spearman (6)
Jerounds Primary Academy, Harlow

The Furry Spider

I have a furry, fluffy head.
I have eight legs.
I have a crawling, big black body.
I have long legs.

What am I?

Answer: A furry spider.

Laci Jensen (5)
Jerounds Primary Academy, Harlow

Butterfly

I have delicate wings that flutter.
I have black antennae that wiggle.
I have an orange body that giggles.

What am I?

Answer: A butterfly.

Malgorzata Sasak (6)
Jerounds Primary Academy, Harlow

Spider

I have a black and orange body.
I have a pincer and large fangs.
I have long, stripy legs.
I am large.

What am I?

Answer: A spider.

Henry James Hughes (6)
Jerounds Primary Academy, Harlow

Butterfly

My beautiful wings are aflutter.
I have beautiful, shiny, pink wings.
They are orange and can glide.

What am I?

Answer: A butterfly.

Amber Bishop (5)
Jerounds Primary Academy, Harlow

Bee

I am yellow and black.
I have a fluffy body.
I have thin wings.
I have dark and spindly black legs.

What am I?

Answer: A bee.

Kirsten Osei-Yeboah (6)
Jerounds Primary Academy, Harlow

Beetle

I have a multicoloured rainbow body.
I walk fast like a bee,
So fast that all you can see is a flash.

What am I?

Answer: A beetle.

Ananya Vyas (6)
Jerounds Primary Academy, Harlow

Butterfly

I am orange and black.
I have a thin body.
I flap my wings and fly.
I can fly in the air.

What am I?

Answer: A butterfly.

Halle Grace Griffin (6)
Jerounds Primary Academy, Harlow

What Am I?

I am cute and cuddly.
I am furry.
I like to play with toys.
I like to chase birds and mice.

What am I?

Answer: A cat.

Harry Cusack (7)
Jerounds Primary Academy, Harlow

Butterfly

I have moonlight black and dark orange wings.
I have wobbly, thin antennae.
I have white dots.

What am I?

Answer: A butterfly.

Pheobe Buckland (6)
Jerounds Primary Academy, Harlow

Snail

I have a round and hard shell.
I have a cold, slimy body with no legs.
Gliding on the ground.

What am I?

Answer: A snail.

Ryan Haddon (6)
Jerounds Primary Academy, Harlow

Snail

I am smelly.
I have a disgusting tail.
I have a brown, soft body.
I am black and shiny.

What am I?

Answer: A snail.

Rose Weber (6)
Jerounds Primary Academy, Harlow

Spider

I have eight legs.
I am bright orange and pitch-black.
My tummy and head are bright yellow.

What am I?

Answer: A spider.

Eddie Kemsley (6)
Jerounds Primary Academy, Harlow

Beetle

I am a shiny rainbow.
I have a black body.
I have a glittering, pretty, skinny antenna.

What am I?

Answer: A beetle.

Millie-Rose Page (6)
Jerounds Primary Academy, Harlow

Butterfly

I have orange wings
Beautiful, orange, shiny wings flying
Small black body flying.

What am I?

Answer: A butterfly.

David Marioara (6)
Jerounds Primary Academy, Harlow

Butterfly

I have small wings that glide.
I have sparkly orange spots.
I delicately flutter.

What am I?

Answer: A butterfly.

Alfie Chappell (5)
Jerounds Primary Academy, Harlow

Worm

I have a slimy body.
I wiggle about.
I am brown and red.
I move through the mud.

What am I?

Answer: A worm.

Dale Gould (5)
Jerounds Primary Academy, Harlow

Spider

I have eight legs and big claws.
I can jump, run and sleep.
I have scary teeth.

What am I?

Answer: A spider.

Harry George James Manoli (6)
Jerounds Primary Academy, Harlow

Bumblebee

I am black and yellow.
I buzz.
I am fluffy and have spindly legs.

What am I?

Answer: A bumblebee.

Evie Joy Pollock (6)
Jerounds Primary Academy, Harlow

Bees

Bees are fuzzy and float.
They are black and yellow,
With stripy, fuzzy legs
And a black body and nose,
Moving so fast.

Noah Daker (6)
Jerounds Primary Academy, Harlow

Worm

I have a skinny body.
I am red and orange.
I have a tail.

What am I?

Answer: A worm.

Jack Downes (5)
Jerounds Primary Academy, Harlow

Butterfly

I have an orange and yellow body.
I fly flower to flower.

What am I?

Answer: A butterfly.

Sophie Savory (6)
Jerounds Primary Academy, Harlow

Butterfly

I have nice orange wings.
I have amazing tiny legs.

What am I?

Answer: A butterfly.

Azeem Idrees (5)
Jerounds Primary Academy, Harlow

Creatures

Spiders bodies are black and green
Worms are slow
Butterflies are fast
Slugs have shiny black bodies.

Caleb Edwards (5)
Jerounds Primary Academy, Harlow

Leopards

Leaping up the trees,
Looking for other animals.
Eating other animals.
Chasing other animals.
Approaching quietly.
Roaring very loudly.
Leopards purring very quietly, looking for other people.
Eating other people.

Jessica Hagger (5)
Jotmans Hall Primary School, Benfleet

Monkey

M onkeys munching on bananas
O oh, ooh, ah, ah
N ibbling on bananas
K icking trees
E ating bananas
Y ay, yippee!

Travis Nunn (6)
Jotmans Hall Primary School, Benfleet

Caiman

C atching other animals
A ttacking fish
I t hunts others
M ighty animals
A ngry creatures
N ice but angry.

James Doré (5)
Jotmans Hall Primary School, Benfleet

Snake

Snakes slithering across the grass in silence.
Down a tree, a snake slithers and eats other animals.
Then silence across the grass.

Dylan Crane (6)
Jotmans Hall Primary School, Benfleet

Snake

Snakes slithering slowly in the grass.
Snakes slowly slithering through the jungle.
Snakes munching other animals up.

Finlay Gow (6)
Jotmans Hall Primary School, Benfleet

Snakes

Snakes slithering slowly
Swirling, saying, "Ssssss."
Slowly swirling across the trees.

Adam David Smith (6)
Jotmans Hall Primary School, Benfleet

At The Toyshop!

I can roll but I don't have legs.
I am inside a huge sphere.
I like to roll about and to get bounced.
I like to get wrapped to see what's inside.

What am I?

Answer: A personalised L.O.L. doll.

Naomi Okafor (6)
Newtons Primary School, Rainham

Out At Night

I can shine bright but I am not the sun.
I come only at night.
I play with my friend, the moon.
You can see me at night.
I am gold and the moon can see me.

What am I?

Answer: A star.

Ioana Rebecca Vencu (6)
Newtons Primary School, Rainham

In The Sea

I have lots of teeth.
I live in the sea but I am not a small fish.
I like to eat fish.
I like to eat humans.
I am grey like an elephant.

What am I?

Answer: A shark.

Muhammad Uzair Khan (6)
Newtons Primary School, Rainham

In The House

I live in your house.
You can build me.
You can put things on me.
I stand still.
I am made of wood.
I can be by the window.

What am I?

Answer: A shelf.

Jason Cibian (6)
Newtons Primary School, Rainham

African Cave

I eat meat.
I live in the jungle.
I do a big roar.
I have sharp claws.
I am a fast runner.
I am not a scary animal.

What am I?

Answer: A lion.

Aaban Master (6)
Newtons Primary School, Rainham

In The Dark

I glow in the dark.
I move very fast.
You can see me at night.
I like going around.
I like going everywhere.

What am I?

Answer: A shooting star.

Tiffany Bevan (6)
Newtons Primary School, Rainham

Teeth

I live in water but I am not a fish.
I have a lot of teeth.
I have bumpy skin.
I am sneaky.
I make animals jump.

What am I?

Answer: A crocodile.

Iya Momprasert (5)
Newtons Primary School, Rainham

In Africa

I am super fast and I go hunting.
I like to sleep in nature.
I don't eat meat.
I have stripes on my body.

What am I?

Answer: A zebra.

Yaqub Sadat (5)
Newtons Primary School, Rainham

In The Woods

I eat meat.
I am not a lion or a tiger.
I live in Africa.
I have sharp claws.
I live in a pack in caves.

What am I?

Answer: A wolf.

Ibrahim Muhammad (6)
Newtons Primary School, Rainham

Flying Beauty

I am beautiful.
I can drink water.
I am colourful.
I love flowers.
I sit in beautiful flowers.

What am I?

Answer: A butterfly.

Leena Follad (6)
Newtons Primary School, Rainham

In The Deep

I have eight legs.
I live under the sea.
I have two eyes.
I have one head.
I have one mouth.

What am I?

Answer: An octopus.

Ashton Waldrum (6)
Newtons Primary School, Rainham

Out In The Sea

I am big like an elephant.
I have a hole to breathe.
I live in the ocean.
I have a big family.

What am I?

Answer: A whale.

Callum Bullman (6)
Newtons Primary School, Rainham

In The Shed

I can fly but I am not an insect.
I lay eggs but I am not a chicken.
I sit on my eggs to keep them warm.

What am I?

Answer: A bird.

Bobby Scott (5)
Newtons Primary School, Rainham

Meteorite

I am hard.
I am made of rock, dust and cement.
I never ever get up.
I am grey and break up.

What am I?

Answer: Concrete.

Joanna Ephrem (5)
Newtons Primary School, Rainham

Shiny And Bright

I am shiny like the sun.
I have five sharp points.
I am shiny at night.
I am high in the sky.

What am I?

Answer: A star.

Isla Summer Leigh Angel Foster (5)
Newtons Primary School, Rainham

Sharp Teeth

I live in the ocean.
I have sharp fins.
I eat people.
I have sharp teeth.
I am grey.

What am I?

Answer: A shark.

Sonny Antonio Pelosi-Davis (6)
Newtons Primary School, Rainham

Spin Webs

Everybody steps on me.
I make webs.
I am black.
I have eight legs.
Nobody likes me.

What am I?

Answer: A spider.

Rishith Saha (6)
Newtons Primary School, Rainham

In A Made Up World

I have a long horn.
I am a rainbow.
I have a long tail.
I am like a horse.
I am made up.

What am I?

Answer: A unicorn.

Ariana Pippa Ramsey (6)
Newtons Primary School, Rainham

What Is On My Head?

I sit on people's heads.
I keep people warm.
I am colourful.
I am fluffy and soft.

What am I?

Answer: A hat.

Somto Ezeofor (5)
Newtons Primary School, Rainham

Outside

I can hop around.
I love carrots.
My tail is fluffy and round.
I live underground.

What am I?

Answer: A rabbit.

Daisy Mae Deitz (6)
Newtons Primary School, Rainham

Wavy

I am blue.
I am wet but not a river.
Some animals live in me.
Boats ride on me.

What am I?

Answer: The ocean.

Tyler Howard (6)
Newtons Primary School, Rainham

Shine Bright

I am shaped like a circle.
I have a head but no hands.
I have a body but no feet.

What am I?

Answer: A coin.

Tasfia Ruhee (6)
Newtons Primary School, Rainham

Weather

I can be scary.
I am cold like rain.
I flash like a light.

What am I?

Answer: A storm.

Seyi Oni (5)
Newtons Primary School, Rainham

White Bones

I am made of bones.
I can scare you.
I am in humans.

What am I?

Answer: A skeleton.

Albie Ramsey (6)
Newtons Primary School, Rainham

Creepy-Crawly

I am big.
I am small.
I am strong.
I make webs.

What am I?

Answer: A spider.

Ayaan Rahman (5)
Newtons Primary School, Rainham

Fireball

I am yellow.
I am hot like lava.
I go away at night.

What am I?

Answer: *The sun.*

Amelia Ho (6)
Newtons Primary School, Rainham

Eating Humans

I am huge.
I eat people.
I have giant fins.

What am I?

Answer: A shark.

Stanley Fitzpatrick (6)
Newtons Primary School, Rainham

The Cheetah

Beside a shiny, cold and clear river, a spotty, yellow cheetah carefully gets a cold drink to get the energy to catch an antelope to eat it.
He silently creeps gently but fast and the fluffy antelope hides behind a smooth, dirty and huge rock.
The antelope goes through a tunnel as hard as a rock, he gets a little cut.
Suddenly, he sees the zooming cheetah.
The antelope tries to run as fast as he can but his cut still hurts.
Suddenly, the scary cheetah bites the poor antelope.

Olaedo Ezinne Ugwoke (7)
Parkwood Academy, Chelmsford

The Cheetah

The spotty, yellow cheetah ran as quick as a shot through the soft, golden sand.
Beside the blue river, a spotty yellow cheetah quietly and quickly had a drink.
Behind an old rock, an antelope with soft but sharp horns hid as quiet as the still wind, from the loud, scary cheetah.

Riley Antony Costello (7)
Parkwood Academy, Chelmsford

The River

Beside the deep and fast river is a soft cheetah waiting quietly to pounce.
He dashes across the burning hot sand as quick as a lightning bolt.
Behind the hard and slimy rocks, a springy antelope silently hides.

Harrison Banes (7)
Parkwood Academy, Chelmsford

The Hippo

The huge hippo splashed and dashed in the long, shining river.
The shimmering river roughly splashed around her.
A dusty can was floating in the river.
She swam softly as soft as a fluffy dog,
Moving carefully.

Thomas Riley Roe (7)
Parkwood Academy, Chelmsford

The Cheetah

The spotty cheetah shot as quick as a rocket onto the boiling hot sand.
The huge elephant ambled past the dirty trees, as loud as a bomb.
The stripy zebra hid as quietly as a mouse from the hungry lion.

Katie Gilbert (7)
Parkwood Academy, Chelmsford

The Hippo

The hippo swam delightfully in the gleaming river.
The gleaming river splashed around him smoothly.
The emerald seaweed floated in the splashing waves.
He glided through the water peacefully.

Summer May Head (7)
Parkwood Academy, Chelmsford

The Cheetah

The speedy cheetah darted in the hot, old desert.
The lumpy sand softly collided around him.
The creaky house crumbled on the dry sand.
The cheetah tiptoed as slow as a snail,
Moving excitedly.

Lucas Herman (6)
Parkwood Academy, Chelmsford

The Monkey

The monkey swings on the old brown tree.
The leaves gently fall down the tree.
In the banana tree, the bananas float around him.
The monkey dashes as fast as a flash, moving cautiously.

Ryan Clayton (7)
Parkwood Academy, Chelmsford

The Cheetah

The fast, spotty cheetah ran across the soft, smooth sand,
He flicked up the sand around him.
In the sand, there was a smooth stone.
The cheetah ran as fast as gunshots, moving quietly.

Finnly Alan Taylor (7)
Parkwood Academy, Chelmsford

The Spotty Cheetah

The spotty cheetah dashes as fast as a roller coaster across the golden sand. Beside the shiny river, a lightning-fast cheetah quickly hides to attack an elephant that wants to drink.

Mikey Robert Mills (7)
Parkwood Academy, Chelmsford

The Elephant

The elephant stomped on the dusty floor.
The dust was flowing gently all around him.
There was a beautiful flower.
He walked slowly like a snail,
Moving peacefully.

Paige Jo Sargeant (7)
Parkwood Academy, Chelmsford

The Rhinoceros

The rhino charged at the old tree.
The green leaves gracefully glided around him.
He stomped on the golden sand as loud as thunder while moving slowly.

Archie Bark (7)
Parkwood Academy, Chelmsford

Football

F ootball is my favourite thing to do.
O ur team is called Finesse, our coach is Ola and he's as strict as a policeman.
O ut we go to play in all weather, my muddy boots get washed by my dad.
T eamwork is so important, we listen and learn and we're just like a family.
B *ang!* A fantastic goal in the top corner. Another one for 'Siddy Goals', that's what they call me.
A ll I want is to be a professional footballer.
L uckily for my big brother, he will be my driver.
L ook out for me in the Premier League.

Sid Albert Ward (6)
Ripple Primary School, Barking

My Sweet Tooth!

My teeth are falling out, my teeth are falling out.
I'm five years old, what could cause my teeth to fall out?
Was it those chewy gummy bears that made my teeth wobble?
The dentist did say that sweets would spell trouble!
Oh no! My school pictures, how will I smile?
A gap between my pearly white teeth,
I'll have to keep my mouth closed for a while.
Even one bite of pizza hurts my tooth,
I can feel the pain as my tooth becomes loose.
I'm going to be a big girl now, with grown-up teeth
And a sparkly smile.

Maryam Imran Mansuri (5)
Ripple Primary School, Barking

Huge Bow

T hey are very cute.
E veryone has many of them.
D o you like the huge bow?
D o you love mesmerising eyes?
Y ou've never seen a fluffy tummy as a pillow.

B oys love them too.
E milija hugged him tightly to her chest.
A sleep in her bed, cuddling a little one.
R emember, always your favourite plaything.
S peak softly and carry a big teddy bear.

Emilija Lagunaviciute (6)
Ripple Primary School, Barking

What Season Am I?

When I arrive, I share my heat.
I need to have ice cream to cool me down.
I visit the sea beach to have fresh air.
Seagulls come and visit me.
I get to wear my dresses.
I have to have a fan on me.
I gather friends and family for a barbecue.
Cold drinks are perfect for this time.
A good excuse to wear my swimming costume.
I go to parks with families to have picnics.

What season am I?

Answer: Summer.

Kanishka Sarkar (6)
Ripple Primary School, Barking

The Fabulous Four

My mood changes throughout the year,
Sometimes I can be hot.
Sometimes I can be cold.
Butterflies and daffodils are my friends.
When it is hot, children love to eat ice cream.
Leaves turn brown and fall off trees,
At the end of the year, people are happy,
Even though it is freezing.
There are four of us.

What are we?

Answer: Seasons.

Ponam Kaur (6)
Ripple Primary School, Barking

A Good Helper

I help people when they are lost.
I can be a man or a woman.
I mostly have a yellow and blue car.
My car makes a loud siren noise.
I arrest bad guys every day.
I carry bad guys to jail for a whole week.
I train special dogs.
I have a dog to sniff bad guys out.

Who am I?

Answer: The police!

Bertille Ashley Okinyi (6)
Ripple Primary School, Barking

The Shark

A big, big shark saw an ark.
He swam to the park and met a boy called Mark.
"Come with me to the dark," said the shark.
"I am not going to the dark, I like to hear the dogs bark.
I can't hear dogs bark in the deep, deep water dark.
Go away shark, I will rest in the park where I can hear the dogs bark."

Ayman Sochi (5)
Ripple Primary School, Barking

Endless Joy Of Spring Multi Colours

April showers bring May flowers.
After lots of April showers,
There are green flower buds one step away
Then multicoloured images bring endless joy.
Buzzing noise makes bees pollinate the flowery trees.
One might be surprised by the fresh, beautiful blanket view.
And not even the white clouds could mess up the universal power.

Hamza Aslam Avram (6)
Ripple Primary School, Barking

My Friend At School

F riends are the best thing about school.
R unning around to play it and playing tag.
I like playing hide-and-seek with my friends.
E very day we laugh together.
N ever will I leave my friend.
D inner time comes and I eat with my friends.
S chool is where I met my friends.

Sariyah Bashar (5)
Ripple Primary School, Barking

My Garden Pets

They live in my garden.
Sometimes they are big and small.
They have stripy, brown coiled shells.
I like to play with them.
I pick them up and they move slowly on my hand.
I like to watch them play hide-and-seek in their shells.

What are they?

Answer: Snails.

Joshua Okine-Williams (6)
Ripple Primary School, Barking

Little Bunny

There is a little bunny,
She is very funny,
She likes to tickle,
And has a cute giggle.
She has long, soft ears
But she has candy tears.
I love her soft fur
And her fine little toes.
Don't go away,
Please stay and play.

Ubaydah Noor (6)
Ripple Primary School, Barking

Riddlin' Unicorn

I go *pop, pop, pop!*
I am white.
I am salty.
I am buttery.
I have to go into the microwave for three minutes.
I am round and pointy.
I am yummy when you watch a movie.

What am I?

Answer: Popcorn.

Alessia-Maria Ciceu (6)
Ripple Primary School, Barking

Your Furry Friend

I sit on your lap.
I like to purr.
I run around the garden.
I could be cute, grey, adorable, mischievous and white and black.
I sometimes scratch but I'm still loved.

What am I?

Answer: A cat.

Hajar Khan (6)
Ripple Primary School, Barking

Santa

S anta Claus will come in the dark night
A nd bring me goodies.
N ext to the Christmas tree,
T omorrow, I will share the presents.
A nd we will sing, "We wish you a Merry Christmas."

Janelle Osei (5)
Ripple Primary School, Barking

Yum Yum

I'm fried and tasty.
I'm served to a lot of people.
I'm part chicken.
I'm small.
I'm hot and spicy.
I'm loved by Aydin.

What am I?

Answer: A chicken wing.

Aydin Bashir (6)
Ripple Primary School, Barking

A Known Animal But Never Seen

I have a yellow horn on my head.
I look like a horse.
I have a white tail.
I have four legs.
I have a lot of white fur.
I have blue eyes and hair.

What am I?

Answer: A unicorn.

Aidan Muhammad Najib (6)
Ripple Primary School, Barking

Strawberry

I see something red.
I taste something sweet, sour and juicy.
I smell something fresh.
I hear it is very healthy.
I feel something soft.

What could it be?

Answer: A strawberry.

Malisa Begum (6)
Ripple Primary School, Barking

Kobby

K obby is my name.
O ften full of praise.
B ecause I am like a maze.
B ecause I blossom in May.
Y oung now and forever ablaze.

Kobby Owusu Ansah (6)
Ripple Primary School, Barking

Butterfly

I'm pink with spots all over.
I eat leaves.
I like to fly.
I start as a cocoon.
I live in the trees in a leafy, friendly jungle.
My wings are sapphire blue.
I have crystal clear diamonds, I am very pretty.
I have furry wings, one is electric blue and the other is rose gold.
I smile when I'm in a flower, my favourite is orchids.

What am I?

Answer: A jungle butterfly.

Ruby Aimee Durrance (7)
St Teresa's Catholic Primary School, Rochford

My Riddle

I have pink stripes.
I am colourful.
I sit around the jungle.
I eat leaves, the big green ones.
I am pretty.
I am really nice to others.
I have pink hair.
I don't like flowers.
My wings are longer than an elephant's trunk.
My wings are giant and colourless.
I blend in everywhere.

What am I?

Answer: A magical butterfly.

Maisie Marshall (7)
St Teresa's Catholic Primary School, Rochford

The Big Cat

I have black stripes and ginger fur.
I have long legs and a strong jaw.
I have padded paws.
I have sensitive whiskers.
I have a long tail.
I have a keen sense of smell.
I have good hearing.
I have a powerful body.
I have a sleek fur coat.

What am I?

Answer: A tiger.

Richard Clarence Henley Harris (7)
St Teresa's Catholic Primary School, Rochford

The Crocodile

I am powerful and speedy.
I live in a warm river.
I have a spiky back.
I have powerful eyes to look at you.
My energy never runs out.
I eat fish and I have sharp, shiny, big teeth
As sharp as a blade.
My skin is as hard as a brick.

What am I?

Answer: A crocodile.

Aidan Ward (7)
St Teresa's Catholic Primary School, Rochford

The Jungle Butterfly

I fly in the sky.
I have beautiful, multicoloured wings.
My wings are as pink as a rose.
I'm a vegetarian.
I fly about in the trees.
I feed on the nectar of jungle flowers.
I'm attracted to water.

What am I?

Answer: A butterfly.

Hannah Masiyambiri (7)
St Teresa's Catholic Primary School, Rochford

The Jungle Butterfly

I have beautiful red, blue and purple wings.
I live in the hot and steamy rainforest.
My wings are a lovely pink and sparkly.
People think my wings are great!
I fly up into the air and I am decorated with sparkles.

What am I?

Answer: A butterfly.

Jessica Morgan (7)
St Teresa's Catholic Primary School, Rochford

A Tiger

I live in the jungle.
I have claws as sharp as a lion's tooth.
My fur is orange and I have dark black stripes.
I have a long tail and I sneak behind big bushes and trees to surprise my prey.
I eat lions.

What am I?

Answer: A tiger.

Ollie Griggs (7) & William Mortonson (7)
St Teresa's Catholic Primary School, Rochford

The Jungle Gorilla

I spend most of the day hunting for fruit roots, bark and leaves to eat.
I spend a lot of the day on the ground.
At night, I climb into the low branches and sleep on beds of twigs.
I chase little boys.

What am I?

Answer: A gorilla.

Zak Collins (7)
St Teresa's Catholic Primary School, Rochford

The Hungry Crocodile

I am green and scaly.
I eat piranha and fish.
I have a great big jaw.
My teeth are as sharp as a needle.
I am strong and big.
I have a long powerful tail.
My favourite food is little boys.

What am I?

Answer: A crocodile.

Quinn Beesley (7)
St Teresa's Catholic Primary School, Rochford

The Toucan

I feed on flowers, nuts and fruit.
I soar and sweep and sit upon the trees.
I have a strong beak.
I have a golden-yellow beak.
I eat juicy berries.
I am black and white.

What am I?

Answer: A toucan.

Amelia Lench (7)
St Teresa's Catholic Primary School, Rochford

The Jungle Chameleon

I have a superpower, I can camouflage.
I have a long, speedy tongue.
I move slowly.
I have a curly tail.

What am I?

Answer: A chameleon.

Ronnie Harvey (7)
St Teresa's Catholic Primary School, Rochford

The King Cobra

I have flaps on the side of my head.
I spit venom.
I am very scaly.
When my skin is dry, it comes off.

What am I?

Answer: A king cobra.

Joshua Tasker (6)
St Teresa's Catholic Primary School, Rochford

Jaguar

I have big claws.
I have a long tail.
I pounce all around the jungle.
I love to pounce on my prey.

What am I?

Answer: A jaguar.

Kai Cundy (7)
St Teresa's Catholic Primary School, Rochford

The Jaguar

I live in the jungle.
I can climb in the trees.
I can swim and eat fish.

What am I?

Answer: A jaguar.

Betsie Mahers (7)
St Teresa's Catholic Primary School, Rochford

Young Writers Information

We hope you have enjoyed reading this book – and that you will continue to in the coming years.

If you're a young writer who enjoys reading and creative writing, or the parent of an enthusiastic poet or story writer, do visit our website www.youngwriters.co.uk. Here you will find free competitions, workshops and games, as well as recommended reads, a poetry glossary and our blog.

If you would like to order further copies of this book, or any of our other titles, then please give us a call or visit www.youngwriters.co.uk.

Young Writers
Remus House
Coltsfoot Drive
Peterborough
PE2 9BF
(01733) 890066
info@youngwriters.co.uk

@YoungWritersUK @YoungWritersCW